BUS STOP

D0243797

Everyone climbed aboard the carpet.

They flew high in the air over Nonsenseland
and Happyland and Coldland
all the way to …

MR. MEN
ADVENTURE IN
Magicland

Original concept by
Roger Hargreaves

Written and illustrated by
Adam Hargreaves

EGMONT

Little Miss Magic had decided to take all her friends on a day out. But she had not told them where they were going.

It was to be a surprise.

The first surprise was when Little Miss Magic turned up at the bus stop on a magic flying carpet.

… Magicland!

Little Miss Magic's favourite place in the world.

"Surprise!" cried Little Miss Magic.

But you will not be surprised to hear that everything in Magicland was magic.

The trees could walk.

The pigs could fly.

The flowers could talk.

Even the air sparkled with magic.

"Everybody," called Little Miss Magic, "I would like you to meet a friend of mine."

They all looked round, but they could not see anyone. Who was Little Miss Magic talking about?

Suddenly, there was a flash and a puff of pink smoke.

"My friend, Wizard Wilf!" she finished, introducing the rather round and jolly-looking wizard who had just magically appeared out of thin air.

"Wizard Wilf is going to be our guide to Magicland," explained Little Miss Magic.

"You don't look like much of a wizard to me," scoffed Mr Uppity, rudely.

"I can promise you I am," said Wizard Wilf.

"Go on, prove it," said Mr Uppity.

Wizard Wilf whipped his magic wand out of his sleeve and muttered some magic words.

With a flash and a bang Mr Uppity turned into a toad.

"Well, you did ask!" laughed Wizard Wilf.

"Now, we have a very long way to go so I suggest that you each put on a pair of these magic boots," said Wilf. "Each step you take in these boots will be bigger than any step you have ever taken and will mean that you can all keep up."

Mr Slow, who usually walks at a snail's pace, could not believe it. Right over a river in one step.

Mr Tall did not need a pair of the boots.

He already has a very long stride!

They all set off, following Wizard Wilf's lead. As they bounded along in their magic boots they came to a field and in the field, was a unicorn.
But that was not all.
There was also a griffin.

And a cow.
A pink Magicland cow!
Mr Rush wanted to know which was the fastest.
So they had a race around the field.
And, of course, Mr Rush won.

After their race they came to a wooden bridge spanning a river, too wide even for magic boots.

"We will have to find another way to cross the river," said Wilf. "An evil troll lives under this bridge and he will eat anyone who sets foot on it."

Wilf pulled out his wand and waved it in the air. "Abracadabra!" he cried.

A rainbow appeared out of nowhere and everyone walked safely over the rainbow to the other side.

The troll was very disappointed.

And then they came to a small, round, jolly-looking cottage.

"This is my house," said Wilf. "We can stop here and have lunch."

Mr Lazy was exhausted and with a sigh he collapsed onto the sofa. But he landed on the floor.

BANG!

"Ouch!" cried Mr Lazy. He could not believe it.

The sofa had moved.

All on its own.

Mr Lazy tried again to sit down.

But this was a Magicland sofa and it had no intention of being sat upon.

When they had their lunch it was also rather messy because all the dishes had run away with the spoons.

After lunch they reached the Blue Mountains. Where the wicked witch lived in a dark and gloomy cave.

"I smell something cooking," smiled Mr Greedy, rubbing his tummy.

There was a large cauldron bubbling on the fire.

But it was a witch's cauldron.

A witch's cauldron full of a magic potion of bats' wings and lizards' tails and beetles and thistles.

"YUK!" cried Mr Greedy as he leaned in over the cauldron.

But Mr Greedy's eyes lit up when he next saw a large shiny red apple in a bowl.

He was about to take a big bite when Little Miss Magic cried, "STOP! That's the wicked witch's poisoned apple!"

"Is there nothing I can eat here?" grumbled Mr Greedy.

Mr Greedy's empty tummy replied with a growl.

And then Little Miss Magic found a cupboard full of the witch's magic brooms.

Everyone went out and played tag.
Flying tag!

Suddenly, the wicked witch arrived with a dreadful rumble of thunder in a great black cloud.

She was in an awful mood.
She scowled and growled and gnashed her teeth.
She shook her fists and screamed in rage.
It was a terrifying sight to behold.

Mr Brave quivered and shook in fear.

But as it turned out, her new boots were too tight.

After a footbath and a cup of tea she was as right as rain.

Not at all wicked.

Although, she did have a rather disagreeable cackle.

It was nearly time to return home, but there was one last thing that Wilf wanted to show them.

He led them into a wood where they found a wishing well.

"If you each throw in a coin," explained Wilf, "then your wish will come true."

Everyone did as he said and made a wish.

Everyone except for Mr Mean.

You would not catch Mr Mean throwing his money down a well!

Little Miss Magic then summoned her magic carpet and they all said goodbye to Wilf.

When they got back home the most extraordinary things began to happen.

Mr Slow was fast.

Mr Sneeze stopped sneezing.

Little Miss Shy was filled with confidence.

And Mr Greedy had the largest apple you have ever seen.

All their wishing well wishes had come true.

Everyone was happy

Everyone except for …

... Mr Mean.

"Bother!" he said, with a deep frown.
"I should have thrown in one coin and wished for two!"